University of Chichester
Bognor Regis Campus
Upper Bognor Road, Bognor Regis
West Sussex PO21 1HR

P
BIR

THE SCHOOL

FANCY DRESS COMPETITION

For Mimi, with love

The author thanks North Waltham
Primary School for allowing him
to show their school in these
pages; but he must emphasise that
the events in this story are
entirely fictitious.

GUMDROP'S
School Adventure

Story and pictures by

Val Biro

h
Hodder
Children's
Books
A division of Hodder Headline Limited

MR JOSIAH OLDCASTLE had a car called Gumdrop. It was his pride and joy – an Austin Clifton Heavy 12/4, vintage 1926. He also had a dog called Horace, a black cocker spaniel. And *he* was Mr Oldcastle's best friend.

One summer's day Mr Oldcastle received a letter from a nearby school.

Dear Mr Oldcastle,

We shall hold a Fancy Dress Competition at our Summer Fair next Saturday, and we would love you to judge the entries. Perhaps you would allow the winners to get a ride in your beautiful car, Gumdrop, as a special prize?

Yours sincerely,
Headteacher

Mr Oldcastle liked visiting schools, so he rang up to say that he'd love to come.

On the Saturday he parked Gumdrop in front of the school, next to a 1911 Darracq. An old fire engine was on display, too, and people admired the gleaming machines.

'Now then, Horace,' said Mr Oldcastle to his dog, 'you stay here and guard Gumdrop.' Horace understood perfectly well, and settled himself on the back seat.

On the playground the fair was in full swing. There was a bouncy castle and a miniature double-decker bus giving rides; there were dogs of every kind getting ready for the best dog competition; a small roundabout, a huge steamroller, a juggling clown and many stalls and stands besides.

There were also children and some grown-ups in fancy dress. Mr Oldcastle saw a pirate, a scarecrow, a Little Bo-peep and a Mad Hatter; a scary witch, a Peter Rabbit and even a little boy in a toy Gumdrop.

He liked them all - though he didn't much care for the man dressed as a robot, nor another as a fat gorilla, who were skulking in the background.

After some thought Mr Oldcastle announced the winners:
'The pirate, Little Bo-peep, and the boy in the toy Gumdrop!
And your special prize is a ride in the real Gumdrop.
Follow me!'
He thought he could hear Horace barking in the distance,
so he hurried along to the front of the school, with the
three children scampering behind.

The Darracq and the old fire engine were still there, and so was the little double-decker bus which had just returned from the playground.

BUT NO GUMDROP! There was no sign of the car. Then Mr Oldcastle realised that he had forgotten to turn off its secret petrol switch. Gumdrop must have been stolen. Horrors!
'Where's Gumdrop?' demanded the children.

This was terrible! His precious car stolen, with Horace
sitting inside it. He must go after them instantly!
Mr Oldcastle required a lift right away, but the
drivers of the Darracq and the fire engine
were both off in the playground.
'My bus here will give you a lift,' said the bus driver.
Well, a double-decker bus, even a miniature one,
was better than nothing, so Mr Oldcastle
squeezed himself half-way up
the stairs. The children
were already on top.

'Hold very tight!'
called the driver,
as the bus lurched forward.

The double-decker bus was a good bus, but not nearly fast enough. By the time they reached the crossroads, Gumdrop and Horace seemed to have disappeared.
'Where's Gumdrop?' wailed the children.
Mr Oldcastle, bouncing on the stairs, moaned miserably. 'We'll never catch them at this rate!'

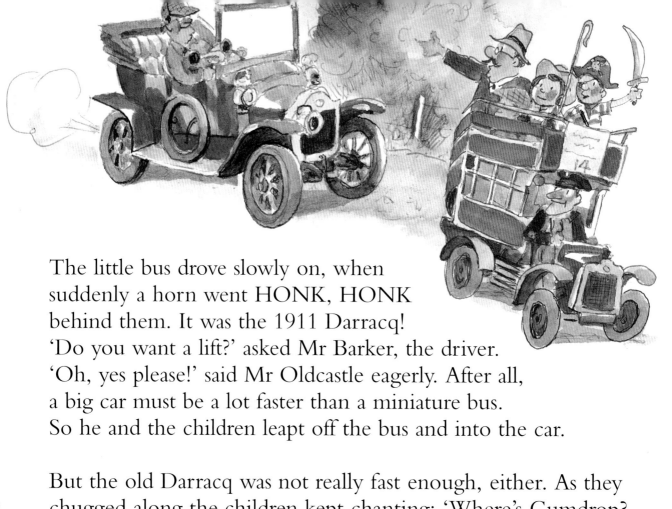

The little bus drove slowly on, when
suddenly a horn went HONK, HONK
behind them. It was the 1911 Darracq!
'Do you want a lift?' asked Mr Barker, the driver.
'Oh, yes please!' said Mr Oldcastle eagerly. After all,
a big car must be a lot faster than a miniature bus.
So he and the children leapt off the bus and into the car.

But the old Darracq was not really fast enough, either. As they
chugged along the children kept chanting: 'Where's Gumdrop?
Where's Gumdrop?' They couldn't
see it anywhere.

When they got to a village, Mr Oldcastle thought that
he could hear a dog barking way ahead. Horace?
But he couldn't say because just then an urgent bell
went CLANG, CLANG behind them.

It was the old fire engine!
'Do you want a lift?' asked the brass-helmeted
driver. Mr Oldcastle accepted gleefully because a fire engine
was surely faster than a 1911 Darracq. 'We shall catch
Gumdrop now!' he cried as he climbed up. The children waved
from the car and wished him good luck.

The fire engine roared through the village, bells a-clanging.
'Where's the fire?' people asked as they jumped for safety.
'Never mind the fire!' shouted Mr Oldcastle.
'Where's Gumdrop?'

At the railway crossing
the lights began to flash,
the barrier came down – and the
fire engine had to stop. And *there* was Gumdrop on the other
side of the crossing, and speeding away!

'Do you want a lift?' asked the driver of the train.
Mr Oldcastle was in such a state that he could hardly think
straight, so he dashed across
and climbed aboard. Anyway,
he thought, a train was
even faster than an old
fire engine.

The train was so fast that
it caught up with Gumdrop in no time.
What's more, Mr Oldcastle saw that the driver was none
other than the gorilla! Yes, the fat gorilla of the Fancy Dress
Competition, with the robot beside him – and there was Horace
in the back, barking fit to burst. This was outrageous!
'Stop! Stop!' cried Mr Oldcastle as they raced along.
'That's my car!'

But to his dismay, the signal ahead changed – so it was
the train that had to stop. Helplessly
he watched as Gumdrop
spurted ahead, turned right
and sped up a farm road.
Mr Oldcastle sprang into
action. He leapt off the
train and sprinted after
his precious car.

But of course it was hopeless. He could never catch Gumdrop on foot. There was no sign of the car – except for a cloud of dust.

Then he noticed a tractor.
'Have you seen Gumdrop?' he asked the farmer in desperation.
'Never mind Gumdrop,' growled the farmer. 'Where's me sheep? They got out and went over that hill there!'
He revved up his engine and Mr Oldcastle just managed to jump on the tractor before it roared off after the sheep.

From the top of the hill they could see it all.
There below was the road. There, too,
were the sheep, blocking the road. And
there was Gumdrop, standing still,
blocked by sheep.

'Now's my chance!' yelled Mr Oldcastle
triumphantly, as he vaulted off
the tractor.

He hopped and skipped down the hill, waving and shouting: 'Stop, thief, stop!' so loudly, that the sheep took fright and scurried away. The tractor followed them in hot pursuit.

Now that the road was clear, Gumdrop shot forward again, churning up the dust.

By the time Mr Oldcastle reached the road,
Gumdrop had gone. All he could hear was
the dwindling sound of an engine and the
distant bark of a dog. Then nothing.
Poor Mr Oldcastle stood there in utter despair.
What chance had he of ever seeing Gumdrop
and Horace again?

Then he heard a voice. 'Do you want a lift?'

Mr Oldcastle's heart leapt when he saw the little green car behind him. It was a 1923 Austin Seven Chummy, and it was driven by none other than his old friend, Mike!
'Yes *please*!' cried Mr Oldcastle and got in.

Now, although the Chummy was a smaller car than Gumdrop, Mike was a better driver than the gorilla. He drove along the twisting farm road so quickly that, sure enough, they soon caught up. There was Gumdrop, just ahead!

'You can't catch me!' shrieked the gorilla and put his foot down. Gumdrop shot forward at such an astonishing speed that the Chummy couldn't keep up.

So Mr Oldcastle stood up in the car and bellowed a command to his dog. 'Horace! STOP GUMDROP!'

The clever dog, who was sitting in the back of Gumdrop, obeyed at once. He squeezed between the gorilla and the robot and pushed in the ignition switch on the dashboard. Then, for good measure, he bit off the button as well.

Gumdrop's engine stopped and the car ground to a halt. The thieves could do nothing about it, so they jumped out and tried to run away. But there was the Chummy, which had just skidded to a stop in front of them.

Instantly, Mr Oldcastle leapt out and grabbed the gorilla; Mike leapt out and grabbed the robot – and Horace leapt about snarling at both.

The thieves were caught and Gumdrop was safe.

Just then a police car drew up, closely followed by the old fire engine and the Darracq with the children. The Inspector of Police looked grim.
'I have reason to believe that we have two notorious vintage-car thieves here whom we've been tracking for ages.'

With that he whipped off the false heads of the robot and the fat gorilla.

'I know these two!' said Mr Oldcastle,
who recognised them instantly.
'That one is Battery Beetle, the car-breaker,
and this is Dyno Dodge, the well-known
scourge of the vintage-car world.'
The Inspector promptly arrested them
both, and the children cheered.

So all was well. Mike had a spare switch for Gumdrop,
so the children got their special ride at last. Above all,
Mr Oldcastle got his old car safely back again –
and clever dog Horace was safe and happy, too.

Then they all drove back to school in triumph. The little
bus came to lead the procession, and when they all
stopped in front of the waiting crowd, a great cheer
went up: 'LONG LIVE GUMDROP!'

First published 2001 by
Hodder Children's Books,
a division of Hodder Headline Limited,
338 Euston Road, London NW1 3HB

Copyright © 2001 Val Biro
ISBN 0340 74977 6 Hardback
ISBN 0340 74978 4 Paperback

10 9 8 7 6 5 4 3 2 1

A catalogue record for this book
is available from the British Library.

The right of Val Biro to be identified as the author
of this Work has been asserted by him in accordance with
the Copyright, Designs and Patents Act 1988.